Dear Father Christmas

Alan Durant

illustrated by

Vanessa Cabban

It was the first of December and the Christmas lights were twinkling in the High Street. Mum took Holly and Billy to meet Father Christmas in the big store. That evening Mum helped Billy write his Christmas list. He left it above the fireplace. But Holly left a letter instead.

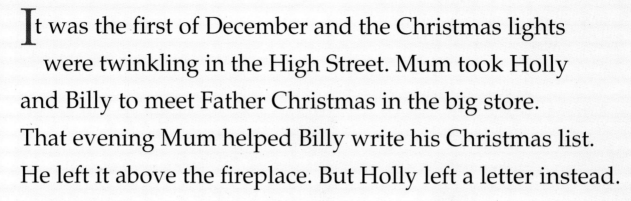

Dear Father Christmas,

I hope you are well. Is it snowing in Lapland? It is cold here.

I saw a man in a shop today who said he was Father Christmas.

He was dressed like you, but was it you? Really? He told me to leave my Christmas list by the fireplace, but I wanted to make sure it really was you.

Please answer.

love Holly

Next morning,
Holly found a letter
addressed to her.

Holly couldn't believe it: a letter from Father Christmas! She knew she should write her list, but there was one really big thing she wanted that she didn't dare ask for. So she wrote again.

Dear Father Christmas,

Thank you so much for your letter. Could you tell me some more about your elves please? How many are there? What do they do? What does Erol look like?

My little brother Billy wants to know if you'll be able to fit his train set on your sleigh. You could probably do with a helper, couldn't you?

Lots of love Holly

PS I hope you like my picture!

Ho HoHo

presents

That night, Father Christmas's elves
went around the world collecting Christmas lists.
One of them found Holly's letter and took
it back to Lapland.

Next morning, there was another letter from Father Christmas by the fireplace.

Holly thought about Erol and the other elves busy in Lapland. She thought about the sleigh and the reindeer too.

She also thought about what she wanted
but still didn't dare ask for it.
I'll write again, she decided.

Dear Father Christmas,
Thank you so much
for your letter and the calendar.
Can you tell me please, what's it like
to ride a sleigh through the sky? How
do you go round the world in just one night?
Wouldn't you like some company? Billy wants
to know how you get down the chimney,
because he says your tummy is quite fat!
With lots of love
Holly
(and Billy)

Father Christmas was having his supper
when Holly's letter arrived.

"Look at this, Billy!" Holly cried
next morning when she opened
her new letter from Father Christmas.

Holly

When Holly put the Christmas
decoration on the tree, she thought about
her list and what Father Christmas
had written. Perhaps if she could
make Erol smile, then she might
dare to ask Father Christmas for what
she really, really wanted…

Holly rushed off to write another letter.

Dear Father Christmas,
I love the decoration. Thank you!
Here is a joke to make Erol smile.
    What's the first thing
elves learn at school?
    The Elf-abet!
What do you do when it isn't Christmas?
Do you always wear red? How do your reindeer
    fly when they don't have wings?
And what do they eat? I would
    LOVE to meet them one day.
    Lots of Love Holly
    PS Do you really
        like mince pies?

Father Christmas was feeding his
reindeer when Holly's letter came. He
hurried back to his grotto to write a reply.

Holly opened her fourth letter.

Holly

As Holly thought about the elves getting the sleigh ready, she knew it was time to ask for what she wanted. If she didn't ask now, it would be too late. That evening she wrote her Christmas list and left it by the fireplace.

At last, it was Christmas Eve. Holly
and Billy hung up their stockings on the
mantelpiece above the fireplace.
They couldn't wait for
Christmas Day. That night,
Holly dreamed
of Father Christmas
setting off on his
journey with
his reindeer.
The elves were
waving and smiling
– even Erol.
Holly dreamed
of the sleigh going
from house
to house,
delivering presents.

Suddenly, Father Christmas was there!
In his hand was a glittering ticket.
"I've brought you your present,"
he said with a smile…

The next moment Holly was sitting next to Father Christmas
in his sleigh on a magical midnight ride
through the snowy starlit sky…

Holly opened her eyes.
The moon was still shining. She saw
an envelope at the bottom of her bed. Inside was
a glittering ticket. So it hadn't just been a dream!
She looked out of the window. Was that Father
Christmas's sleigh she could see, racing across
the sky to Lapland? Yes, she was sure it was!

"Thank you for making my wish come true,
Father Christmas," she breathed.
"Happy Christmas!
See you next year!"